# SHMELF the Hanukkah Elf

Greg Wolfe  illustrated by Howard McWilliam

BLOOMSBURY
NEW YORK LONDON OXFORD NEW DELHI SYDNEY

First published in the United States of America in September 2016
by Bloomsbury Children's Books
www.bloomsbury.com

Bloomsbury is a registered trademark of Bloomsbury Publishing Plc

For information about permission to reproduce selections from this book, write to
Permissions, Bloomsbury Children's Books, 1385 Broadway, New York, New York 10018
Bloomsbury books may be purchased for business or promotional use. For information on bulk purchases please contact
Macmillan Corporate and Premium Sales Department at specialmarkets@macmillan.com

Library of Congress Cataloging-in-Publication Data available upon request
ISBN 978-1-61963-521-0 (hardcover)
ISBN 978-1-61963-523-4 (e-book)   •   ISBN 978-1-61963-524-1 (e-PDF)

Art drawn with pencil on paper and then painted digitally
Typeset in Windsor BT
Book design by Jessie Gang
Printed in China by Leo Paper Products, Heshan, Guangdong
1 3 5 7 9 10 8 6 4 2

All papers used by Bloomsbury Publishing, Inc., are natural,
recyclable products made from wood grown in well-managed
forests. The manufacturing processes conform to the
environmental regulations of the country of origin.

For Julie and Connor: I love the holidays, but I love the two of you even more

—G. W.

For Rebecca and our two little elves, Rufus and Miles

—H. M.

Up at the North Pole, covered in snow,
You'll find Santa's workshop, as most of you know.

But no one can do all that work by themselves—
So helping him out is his army of elves.

The most unsung elves of those who assist
Are the elves in charge of checking The List.

They all work so hard, down to the last elf,
And the newest of them was a fellow named Shmelf.

Shmelf didn't spend time
Playing merry elf games,
But sat in his cubicle,
Staring at names.

His job was to check
Through Santa's List twice,
To see whether kids
Had been naughty or nice.

Shmelf *loved* what he did!
But as Christmas drew near,
He looked at his list,
And he cried out, "Oh, dear!"

He'd found many children
Who *had* been quite good
But would not receive presents,
Though it seemed that they should!

He ran like a flash to see the head elf,
Who smiled and said, "Now, now, calm yourself, Shmelf!
Of course you don't know, since you're still quite newish,
But the kids on this list are actually Jewish."

"They don't celebrate Christmas,
But that's fine, you see . . .
They celebrate Hanukkah,
Their own jubilee.

It won't be dear Santa
Who brings them a gift
But their mommies and daddies.
Do you get my drift?"

Shmelf returned to his desk; his mind was quite shaken—
"Kids with no Christmas? He must be mistaken!"

So later that night,
    careful not to be missed,
He snuck off to visit
    a house on the list.

Shmelf peered in and wondered, Could this be right?
There wasn't a tree or a stocking in sight!

Instead he saw menorahs with candles so thin,
And children were giving their dreidels a spin.

There was gelt—chocolate coins
wrapped up in gold foil,

And latkes frying
in pans filled with oil.

Then Shmelf saw there *were* presents—one for each night!
His elfish eyes gleamed as he squealed with delight.

Shmelf listened as Mom told the Hanukkah story
Of the Maccabees' battle for Israel's glory.
And though the brave soldiers won their great fight,
Their temple had oil for just one more night.

But once they'd set the oil ablaze,
A miracle happened! It lasted eight days!

"Hey, now I get it!" Shmelf said with a grin.
"Hanukkah's awesome! I'm totally in!"

He raced back north and went straight to The Boss,
The big man himself, good old Santa Claus.
Shmelf explained his discovery, this holiday grand—
And when he was done, Santa held up his hand.

"Good Shmelf," chuckled Santa, "it fills me with joy
To see how you care for Jewish girls and boys.
It shows me that you are much more than a clerk,
And so, I will task you with this special work:"

"Hanukkah is a time for family and song,
For joy and tradition—it's where you belong!
I've decided: at Hanukkah you'll travel the world,
Bringing magic and joy to each boy and each girl."

Santa gave Shmelf clothes of white and of blue
(The colors of Hanukkah—that much Shmelf knew) . . .

And a sleigh that could soar straight through the air,
With a Jewish reindeer by the name of Asher.

Now, you good Jewish kids,
    for eight nights each December,
Shmelf will come visit
    (some years in November).

He'll make sure your latkes are crispy and thin,

Your menorahs burn brighter,

and your dreidels win.

If there's one special gift that you'd like this year,
Tell Shmelf—he'll whisper in Mom's or Dad's ear.

He'll do what he can to nudge them that way,
In hopes that the present brings
cheers of "Hooray!"

To reward Shmelf and Asher for all their good will,
You can leave out some gelt and a nice kosher dill.

*What a magical Hanukkah!* you'll think to yourself . . .

See you next year, Shmelf the Hanukkah Elf!